C000101592

THE JOB

A CAL OAKENFLAME ADVENTURE

JOSHUA RAMEY-RENK

Copyright © 2024 by Joshua Ramey-Renk

All rights reserved.

No part of this book may be reproduced or transmitted in any form or by any means, electronic or mechanical, except for the purpose of review and/or reference, without explicit permission in writing from the publisher.

Cover design copyright © 2024 by Kelley York
sleepyfoxstudio.net

Published by Water Dragon Publishing
waterdragonpublishing.com

ISBN 978-1-962538-43-5 (Trade Paperback)

FIRST EDITION

10 9 8 7 6 5 4 3 2 1

AUTHOR'S NOTE

I'm a fan of urban fantasy, post-apocalyptic futures and imagining the place where I live as some future landscape when the world has moved on and there is magic afoot ... I think Cal and Petra are just the heroes for that kind of adventure.

THE JOB

CAL'S HORSE HAD HAD ENOUGH. Copper was normally as patient as they come, but after the long trek through what had been the big highway between old San Jose and New San Fran the mare was done with his nonsense.

With Seven-Mile House having been burned down in some raid or another, the food and shelter along the journey had been subpar for both of them and a day of rain had made the usually well-packed dirt a dangerous mud pit for miles. Even the minor drying enchantment Cal had surrounded them with wasn't much help-it could barely keep up with the amount of water coming out of the sky; it was like riding his horse through a steam bath fully clothed. While it was warm, it was incredibly uncomfortable for both man and horse.

As they picked their sodden way into the tiny hamlet of Harrison, Copper headed straight to where she could smell other horses, in spite of his attempts to keep her heading down the main street to see what options there were for food and a dry bed. The woman at the livery gave him a smile as he slid off the saddle, and pointed out the hotel across the way from where they were.

"How far to Frisco?" Cal asked, hoping to eke out the lay of the land. He had arrived at his destination with no plans to keep heading north, but making conversation with the locals was always a good way to hear the best gossip. He was surprised by her snort of derision. She fixed him with a steady gaze and raised an admonitory finger.

"Never call it Frisco, cowboy. Not unless you want people to know you aren't from anywhere around here. Not like that's not obvious anyway." She pointed at the silver buckles on his gear, forged into the sigil of the mage's college further south.

"Guess you're not a cowboy after all, Not much call for your kind out here." Her cool blue eyes studied him. "We tend to keep ourselves to ourselves." She moved the finger to point across the street, a clear dismissal. "Best get over there before they run out of food. Should be plenty of hooch at least."

•　　•　　•

Later, having finally dried off and had a meal and a nap, Cal made his way to the meeting hall, made obvious by its grand presence right at the top of the main street, commanding a view of the whole town. At the college, they'd studied the several centuries of Lifor history, and Cal could see the outlines of the ancient military settlement that were the bones of Harrison.

A large public square had once taken up the rest of the top of the main drag, but all that remained were a few broken bits of the adobe wall along its outline, slowly returning to the mud it had been formed from centuries ago. His boot heels were loud on the whitewashed boards of the meeting house's porch, and the bracelets at his wrists gave a slight buzz as he crossed the open threshold. Nothing too serious, this was an open public meeting house and he was there for a purpose, but somebody had set up a few hastily rigged alarms that could be switched on with a word or two. "Nightwatchman stuff," the headmaster at Peregrine House called that sort of charm, "Keeps out the drunks and the bums."

The meeting was already in full swing when he walked in, and he hung a little to one side in the back of room to get the lay of the land. He could tell even from the backs of the attendees that this little valley town had the usual mix of storekeepers, cowboys, and politicians, along with the expected range of well-off and working folk. What surprised him was the man currently speaking, his white shirt and black collar the mark the Paulist order, a strong church in much of the world but relatively rare in Lifor. He must be trying to establish a new chapter house.

"And it's through prayer and submission that we will be saved from these predations," the man said, "Not through show of force or negotiation. We must repent and ask St. Paul to intercede for us through his savior in heaven." There were a few laughs, but also a few sounds of agreement. "These bandits are sent from the devil himself to punish us for wickedness!"

A woman with her brown curls restrained by a workingman's hat stood up, and Cal recognized her as the livery attendant. "I don't know about that," she said. "But I'm fairly certain my lambs didn't get taken by no devil — unless he rides a horse and laughs as he snatches them up and disappears up the canyon. That's just a bandito stealing my flock for his own supper pot. Besides, we already got a plan."

There was more laughter, and the Paulist grew red-faced as he readied his retort. Cal knew the Paulists weren't really big on their women folk speaking up.

Cal took that as his cue. It wasn't just an occasional lamb that was going missing, otherwise he wouldn't be here. He hoped he made a suitably competent impression as he strode up the middle of the hall and wasn't above muttering a cantrip that made his oiled duster flare out behind him as if he was striding through a mighty windstorm. "I hear," he said, conversationally, "Somebody called for a mage?"

·   ·   ·

"How are you going to find them?" That was Harrison's mayor, Tom, who had originally asked Peregrine House for help. He had spent a fair amount of the town's limited funds on the message orb, but the House had refunded half of it when they found out this was about missing livestock. "We've had searchers cast out that way, but there's nothing but coyotes and dust."

Cal grimaced. He'd already met the town's sheriff and was surprised the man could muster up the energy to fall off his stool at the saloon, let along gather enough spirit to launch effective seekers.

"With all due respect, this is a bit bigger than your man has had to deal with in the past. I'm working on it, but I think I have a way." Tom nodded and tossed back the whiskey he'd had the bartender pour them from his private stash behind the bar.

"Alright, lemme know if you need anything from us."

Cal knew there was only one person he'd met so far that he'd be asking for help from. Besides, he needed to check on Copper.

•   •   •

Cal squinted into the alkali dust kicked up by the wind blowing into the canyon between him and the range of hills he was guessing hid the bandit camp. It was a maze of canyons and ridges, but that's where he had to be if he was going to take care of the job the townsfolk had hired him for.

He slid down the scree face to where he'd seen the slim figure dismounting, and nearly crashed into Petra Everheart as the loose rock made regaining his balance trickier than he planned. Petra laughed at his undignified descent and he grinned back at her. He'd been told about the plan she and a couple of locals had cooked up, but had doubts.

"Here," she said, "if you can stand up long enough to read it." She handed him the roughly printed poster. "Aunt Lainie had the boys at the print shop make this up."

It wasn't a great likeness, but the face under the "WANTED" text looked passably like Petra, if she had an eye patch and a moniker.

"Sharp Shooting Sally?" Cal raised an eyebrow at Petra. "Really".

She snatched back the paper. "Who says I ain't? Da taught his baby girl how to hit a squirrel's eye at fifty yards. Besides, I needed to sound outlaw-y. Picture could be better, but we were rushed."

Cal made a gesture and the copper bracelets warmed as the features on the poster re-arranged themselves — now they looked both more and less like the woman in front of him. He glanced at her and then back at the image. Then at her again. Especially at her chest, which was a bit more ... human proportioned ... than the picture. Maybe it was the gingham dress with its modest lace bodice.

"You just leave those as they are in that there picture, cowboy. A girl has to have some mystery about her." She tucked the picture back into her saddle bag. Cal couldn't understand the nickname she'd given him the first day he met her, but she seemed stuck on it. It sounded better than "mage boy", so he let it go. He was doubly sure their too-clever-by-half plan was doomed to fail, but kept silent about his own solution to the problem.

Cal looked up at the sun, a fierce flame just over the rim of the canyon. "It'll be dark soon. Let's get back to town." He swung up into Copper's saddle and Petra mounted her own mare, the mellow Suki. She kicked the horse into motion behind Copper and they headed out of the box canyon toward town.

Unnoticed, dark eyes watched their departure, then a shadowy shape made its way up to the bandit camp ...

•　　•　　•

Petra was in her broad sun brimmed hat in the garden when she heard hoofbeats. Instinctively, she gripped the long wooden handle of the hoe she was using to thin out the radishes, but relaxed when she recognized Copper. She couldn't make out the rider, but it looked the right size and shape to be Cal, so she put down the tool and waved a greeting. He was coming up pretty fast, but maybe it was a chance to let Copper run a bit after a couple of days in the stable.

The smile of welcome died on her face when she realized the rider was masked, and carried a wide bullwhip at their side — this wasn't Cal. Before she could shout a warning to her aunt inside, the rider was on her, and the whip lashed around her feet, dropping her to her knees. She groped for the hoe, determined not to be an easy bandit target, but the rider's momentum had already carried them past her and to the end of the braided strip of rawhide. She yelped as she was jerked forward and dragged along several yards, her muslin dress sparing her knees the worst of the scraping. Copper whinnied, braced as the rider hopped off, and Petra rolled to a stop right behind the mare's tail.

Before she could catch her breath, the rider had her bound and blindfolded and hauled up behind him like a calico flour sack, and all she could do was hope she didn't fall off as the traitorous horse and rider fled with their captive into the hills.

•   •   •

The passage of time was a blur to Petra, reduced to the bouncing and jarring and indignity of being trussed and carried into the foothills for what felt like hours, although the day was still hot. She passed out for a time, which she considered a mercy, and eventually woke up to the sound of voices.

A raspy one that she figured was the Rider, and a low murmur that seemed several feet away from wherever Copper had stopped. She took comfort in the horsey smell of Cal's ride, and wondered what had happened that the mare was being ridden by somebody else. Some help he was if they could steal his horse from right under his nose.

There were other smells in the air, and not as pleasant as leather and saddle soap coming from the horse. Bad cooking and unwashed bodies were what her nose was picking up, and her heart started beating fast when she realized she was probably in the bandit camp that the people in her village had been hunting for unsuccessfully. If she could escape, she could get home and bring back villagers, maybe even Cal, if he was still alive after whatever they had done to him to steal Copper.

A rough tug pulled her off the horse and she wobbled as she tried to find her feet. How long had she been out? How far had they travelled? Could she find a way home?

She still couldn't make out the conversation, the hood muffled the words, but she felt a hand pawing at her bodice and a rough laugh when she shrank away. Another grip on her hair, and she was pushed forward this time, stumbling on unsteady feet toward … wherever they were forcing her to go.

Suddenly the air was cooler, and she realized she must be in a room or a building. She felt herself pushed to her knees and bent over what felt like a rough mattress, from the rustling she knew it must be filled with corn husks. More conversation, another hand trying the laces on her bodice, then the sound of a rough blow, an objection followed by more laughter, then a scuffle, a door slamming, and silence. She felt more than knew that there was somebody in there with her, and it was confirmed when she was pulled to her feet and the raspy voice from behind her said loud enough to be heard through the thick hood, "Scream."

The gag was loosened, and she took a shuddering breath. "What do you mean, scre—"

Her arm was twisted behind her back, not painfully but she knew it could become that in a heartbeat.

Raspy voice spoke again. "Scream, like you mean it". Slightly more pressure on her wrist, more a promise than an injury. And she felt her skirts being pushed up from behind.

Petra obliged, launching a shriek that let her get some of her nerves under control. "Good," said Raspy, "Again."

She screamed again and heard even more laughter from outside ... wherever they were.

"Good. Now. If you want to live, keep quiet!"

The hood came off and she blinked even though the room was dim. She could feel the breath from the bandit who had taken Cal's horse. He still held her arm locked behind her, and she felt him doing something she couldn't see.

But there was one thing she could hear. The familiar faint clink of beaten metal bracelets.

Before she could speak again, a hand moved over her mouth and Raspy said, "Do. Not. Speak." He held his hand there until he felt her nod, then released her and stepped away. She whirled unsteadily, and came face to face with Cal. Who quickly grabbed her and placed his hand over her mouth again as she almost said his name.

His mistake.

She bit down on the fingers holding her quiet, and he cursed. But he didn't let her go, just tightened his grip so she couldn't get her mouth open again. "By all the Gods, will you keep quiet? Do you want us both killed?" His voice was a raspy hiss that wouldn't carry outside.

Petra glared daggers that Cal felt even in the dark room. He rubbed the fingers where she had bitten him and winced when she hissed right back at him, "This wasn't the plan!"

She was right. Her plan had been simple. By creating the Wanted posters, Petra and the town council had thought that they would be able to find a way to ally with the bandits and found out the location of their camp. But Cal knew that the fake "Sharp Shooting Sally" would probably never pass as an actual bad guy (or gal, Cal amended mentally), but he went along with the plan until he could make a better one. He'd have to hope that she'd understand once it was all clear — her teeth were sharp!

Shaking out his bruised digits, he gestured Petra over to where a length of badly tanned rawhide served as a curtain for *whatever* this room was. Petra was starting to think of it as a *lair*, but that seemed too grand. *Hovel* was where she landed, nodding to herself internally once she had the word that described the dirt floor, the poor mattress, and the bad window treatments. Her Da had always said she liked words too much, but Aunt Lainey was a Bookwoman, and had praised her growing up for wanting to name things just right.

Cal pulled the curtain just the slightest bit to the side, and Petra could see a group of people around a bright fire, passing around a bottle and a woman or two being passed around in about the same manner.

"See anybody you recognize?" Cal asked, and she dared to look a little more, hoping that the firelight would keep the other's attention or at least their vision away from the hovel where the two were peeking from. She didn't see anybody she knew at first, but then she recognized that there was one person who wasn't handling either the drink or the women. She drew in a sharp breath.

"That's the Preacher!"

Cal nodded and drew her away from the window. "Yep, that what's I thought too. Now, what do you suppose he's doing here?

Petra realized that something else had to be cleared up first. "You!" Her whisper didn't mask the fury in her voice, "What the dang were you thinking? You could have killed me!"

Cal took a half step back, making sure he was out of snapping range. He risked a grin "I had to make sure you were really scared. This place has been hidden by a very strong casting, so I could only break it if I was really doing something bad."

"Bad? You owe me a new dress!" She pulled up the ends of her dress and pointed to where the cloth had torn when she was dragged. "And some new skin!" She showed him the scrapes on her now-revealed knees, and then blushed and pushed her dress back down to proper modesty. "And don't look at me like that!" She was glad the darkness hid her reddening cheeks.

Cal couldn't help but grin. He'd wrapped her in a *byssum* spell as he was riding up, and the minor scratches were less than she could get on a given day working with her livestock. But her sudden shyness was sweet. "We'll talk about that later — now, I need you to scream again.

Eyes blazing, and cheeks burning, she obliged.

•   •   •

Cal had known they could never find the bandit camp without actually being a bandit somehow. At the Mages' college he had always been impressed with how much time bad people put into malignant castings and conjurations, the oddly named *Mudders Map* among them. Apparently named after some long-ago fictional magick, *Mudders* made a location all but impossible to locate unless one was actively committing a crime or had committed so many it was almost as if being a criminal was a core part of the soul. The work and effort it took to hide a *Mudder* was tremendous, and Cal's instructors had often bemoaned the fact that talent to do that would be much better spent helping Lifor society rather than contributing to its troubles.

Right now, Cal was less concerned with the moral debates within magick and far more interested in what a Paulist minister was doing in this den of baddies. It would have made sense if he'd been trying to convert them or was giving a sermon preaching, but it looked like he was here as a guest somehow. And if he knew where the camp was ...

"He's bad," said Petra in her softest voice. "For all his talks about good works, he is just like any other bandit." Cal was about to agree, but at that moment Copper chose to move her position to block their view. He took advantage of the loss of line of sight to close the curtain and pull Petra back into the shadows of the hovel.

"Here's what we do next," Cal started to say. But Petra butted in.

"He's bad, and we gotta tell the town! They are about to let him build a church in the right in the middle of Harrison and start taking tithes from everybody!"

This was normal procedure — established Paulist churches collected a small amount of trade from each citizen in a town they were established, and in exchange looked after the spiritual welfare of the people. They were also supposed to supply a moderate level of health and educational services, but as often as not that meant a fairly poor bargain for the people. Cal preferred the hedge schools, run mostly by women who tended to think about the needs of the community and who weren't afraid of magick. Paulists tended to be a little literal in the interpretation of their book, although it was masked in "saving souls" when they drove mages out of a community or closed down hedge schools because their book said that witches should not be suffered to stay.

"Yep, and we will. But we have to do it right. Can you walk?" Petra stamped her feet at him to let him know his question was a little ridiculous and danced a little jig to take the sting out of it, flinging her arms up and spinning with an exasperated eye-roll. Cal grinned. "Good, get ready to run. But first, take this."

He slipped a small ring onto her right middle finger. It was warm and too loose at first, but after a moment it fit perfectly. "This will let you ride Copper home. Get there as fast as you can and grab the village posse. Then wait for me at your farm."

She nodded and was about to say something when he continued. "And, I'm sorry for this." Before she could react, he reached out and with a quick wrench, tore the top of her bodice down to her shift, then in a motion dropped his trousers to his feet. He pointed to the door "Get on Copper and GO! You've just escaped losing your honor to a baddie, now act like it!"

"You ain't heard the last of this, Cal Oakenflame!" Petra hissed, and dashed out the door, leaping onto the horse, who seemed to be waiting for her. Cal stumbled after her, more clumsy than she would have thought, his feet twisted up in his drawers. He grabbed at her, missed, fell flat, and she was away on the mare before he could find his feet.

The last thing she heard as she fled was an uproar of laughter from the bandits at the misfortunes of the would-be kidnapper who couldn't keep a hold of his victim.

After a suitable ersatz effort to reach Petra, mostly making sure she'd gotten clear of the firelight, Cal rolled back into the dark room and slammed the door. The job was taking a little more out of him than he expected; his dignity was not the least of the damages he was taking to take on Harrison Township's bandit problem. Still, he reflected as he pulled up his trousers and set himself to rights, it did have some redeeming qualities.

While he made it a practice not to look at skin that wasn't being shown to him, Petra *had* offered up a pleasant view of her legs, and her shoulders were lovely under the bodice he'd had to damage. *Enough of that*, he scolded himself as he contemplated his escape plan. Now that he'd been in the camp, he would have an easier, but not totally simple, way to find it in the future. But without Copper to take him out of the hills, he wasn't sure which way town was, or how far off.

He sighed, and got busy.

First, dirty as the floor was, he lay down and scrunched himself under the bed for a working. Spitting on his thumb, he traced a sigil on the underside of the bare boards that supported the scratchy mattress. It flared briefly, then with a slight smell of charred wood winked out, leaving behind a faintly scorched outline of the rune.

Cal figured the odds of anybody cleaning *under* the bed were small, and even a *Findout* enchantment would have small chance of revealing the marks, since they were out of sight and below eye-level. A competent mage would think to look there, but Cal felt like this gang's higher level magick budget had been blown on the *Mudders Map*. Besides, he wouldn't give them an excuse to look very hard.

Second, he twisted one of the bracelets he wore three times around his wrist and uttered a few words, activating the connection between it and the ring he'd given Petra. It wasn't a great *Pathfinding* working, but the *Hot/Cold* casting would let him at least get some general bearings in the dark.

He sighed again. In the dark, *on foot. In unknown territory. It could be worse* he thought, as he wrapped the silk of the mask back around his face, preparing for his next move, *it could be raining.*

He burst out of the hovel, the suitable picture of a thwarted bully, still appearing to be pulling back on his hastily removed clothing. "Which way," he rasped, sticking to the shadows outside the firelight. "Which way did the wench go?"

One of the drunk women cackled and pointed her bottle toward a slight footpath. "Go get 'er, tiger!" she slurred. "A real Romo, you are!" The other woman laughed as well, then yelped as one of the poorly dressed men grabbed her and pulled her down for a kiss.

Cal limped down the path, grateful that there was no honor among thieves or their slatterns, and he made it several hundred yards down the trail before the first drops started falling from the skies.

At least the bracelet was warm, so he was heading in the right direction.

•　　•　　•

After finally getting back into Harrison to discover that his horse had been put away and was drier and warmer than he was, Cal finally found the respite of his room at the inn. He assumed that Petra had made it back to her farm after stabling Copper, and he was too exhausted to do more than strip off his wet clothes and collapse onto the quilt on top of the bed.

He hadn't done any mget,r workings, but keeping up the various small ones, Petra's ring, his pathfinding bracelet, and the runework at the camp had been enough to make him have to choose between being dry or staying warm on the way back, and he'd chosen warm, since there's only so wet you can get and he didn't know how long he'd be walking in the rain.

He still didn't know how long it had been, other than that it was not yet dawn and he was exhausted.

His last bit of energy was an *Alurums* charm on the head of the stairs a few yards in front of his door, but not a big one. After all, he had been invited by the town council. Then nothing but the darkness behind his eyes.

Which didn't last nearly long enough.

There must have been several of them, and they weren't sneaking, because the *Alarums* went off in his ear just as the pounding started on his door. And it wasn't subtle.

"Open it up, mage, we know you're in there! Time to face your sins!" He recognized the voice of Alton, the town's sheriff.

While Cal was certain he had plenty of sins, there weren't any that were any of Alton's, or the town's, business. But his eyes were open and the room's light told him it was at least morning, so he roused himself.

"Easy there! I'm coming." He dashed some cold water on his face, checked his bracelets (still not recharged, but he had them), and pulled his trousers up. Not the first time he'd had to dress in a hurry in an inn, but usually it nothing to do with sheriffs or town councils.

The pounding continued, and Cal took a moment to clear the last of the fog from his head. He also took the time to make sure he knew where the best path to the window was in case he needed an exit in a hurry. He'd have to hope he'd have time for a *Byssum* on the way down to the ground if it came to that.

Finally, he opened his door, and tried to put on the very best Offended Powerful Mage air he could. It worked, a little, and the four men outside on the landing at least didn't try to rush the room. Alton was in front, and said formally, "Master Oakenflame, you are bound

17

to law. We have serious accusations that you have created much mischief here, and that you are the cause of our troubles, not the solution. Please put these on."

Alton dangled a pair of finely wrought silver and iron bracelets, which would both prevent Cal from accessing his magick and render him physically weak.

"I don't think I will," he said, trying to elevate the Angry Wizard façade.

"You will or you damn yourself by disobeying a lawful command!" That voice came from the back of the small group. Of course. The Paulist minister was mixed up in this. Cal started to worry a bit more than he had before.

"That's right," said another of the men, "Preacher says he saw you with the bandits, forcing yourself on one of our womenfolk."

Godsdamn it. He hadn't been as careful as he thought while in the bandit camp. But this was easy to get around. "And who was this woman?"

"Petra Everheart, and she ain't been seen since her aunt says she was snatched up by a rider yesterday."

Well, that wasn't good.

•　　•　　•

As they walked toward the meeting hall, in addition to wondering where Petra had gone, Cal kept pondering two facts over and over. Why was the Preacher in the bandit camp, and how had that ragtag group of drunken criminals been able to afford such a complex conjuring as the *Mudders Map* to hide the camp? He couldn't get rid of the notion that the two were connected. But how?

He didn't like the feeling the bracelets gave him, but the good news was that as his Peregrine House instructors had taught him, the best way to be treated like a mage was to act like a mage. He kept his pace quick and determined, as if he was the one leading the way, not his captors, and a grim expression on his face was meant to communicate that he was very not amused by being dragged from his bed by the yokel constabulary.

•   •   •

Petra woke up in the dark, surrounded by the smell of damp, and ... hootch? She managed to stand, wobbling a bit as her bound hands kept her off balance and tingling told her that she'd been out long enough for her legs to cramp up under her. The last thing she remembered was putting Copper away in the stable and latching the door behind her. Then ... a sound? Footsteps? A tingling feeling not unlike what her legs felt now? Then nothing.

Now this. Someplace that smelled like the bad booze they served in the saloon in town, and cellar damp. It wasn't usual for places in Harrison to have cellars, but she knew a few people and shops had them for storage, so she wondered if she was under some kind of business. She took a tentative step forward in the darkness and cursed when she nearly fell after discovering that her feet were hobbled too. Some kind of rope with just enough play to let her take small steps, which is why she hadn't noticed at first as she had gotten up.

That's enough of that, she thought. Her hands were tied, but they were tied in front of her, and she slowly felt her way to a wall — *rocks, big ones*. Sliding down so she could sit, she stretched her legs out in front of her.

She couldn't see a thing but was flexible enough to reach the hobble on one foot and get her fingers around the knot.

It was not an expert job, and Petra had done enough work with wet bridles and lead ropes to have fairly nimble fingers, even with her hands bound together. *Whoever did this never had to get a lamb out of that briar tangle up on the ridge.* It took time, but eventually her feet were free. She'd worry about her hands later. For now, she wanted to figure out where she was without falling down.

Moving carefully, she paced the room, ultimately figuring out it was some kind of storage cellar. She could feel a few shapes of that felt like wooden boxes, or chests. Eventually she felt what could only be a door, and gingerly tested the latch. *Locked, of course.* She considered screaming — she'd had enough practice at that recently but decided against it. *Someone knows I'm here ... the dirty critter that put me here! No need to let them know I'm awake. Not yet.*

Eventually she had circled the strangely shaped room twice and returned to the chests. She had found a sharp edge of rock to take care of the restraints on her wrists on her second pass and used her newly-freed hands to explore the containers a little more thoroughly. The first held only some kind of empty bottles, the second had the same bottles, but heavier, so she figured they must be full versions.

The third was harder to open, but she eventually was able to raise what she assumed was the lid. Inside were some kind of hard metal shapes, a dozen or more by her count. Her fingers traced their edges, and they made her think of small loaves of bread as she explored their outlines. On several, she could feel some kind of design pressed into the metal, and it rang a slight bell in her mind. She picked one up, noting that it was heavy for its size. Then she gasped.

The box was full of gold.

•   •   •

The Preacher watched the little group of townsfolk usher the blaspheming mage into the meeting hall and double checked his surroundings. He had split off from the group once they had the chains on the man called Cal and he was convinced that he was out of the way for a while. He moved around back to the back of the saloon, where another cloaked figure was waiting for him.

"It's a good thing you saw them when you did," said the newcomer, "otherwise we might not have known who to look for. You were right, she didn't look like her picture."

The Paulist snorted and said in a sanctimonious tone, "And we know which parts you were looking at, *magician*."

Now the newcomer snorted in turn. "Doesn't your book tell you not to judge? And to render unto the man what is his?"

"You'll get your gold," the Paulist clutched his book as if it could ward off any threat the newcomer posed. "It worked out well to have those criminals stealing so much livestock. We will almost make a profit from this endeavor, even before the town asks us to set up a permanent chapter here. And then," a fervent note crept into his voice, "we'll finally be able to start ridding this part of Lifor of the likes of the Hedges, and *you*."

The stranger laughed, "Makes no difference to me what you do, just as long as I get paid. It took a lot of resources to hide that camp from the town, and it got worse once Oakenflame showed up. I want the girl too."

The Preacher shrugged. That solved a problem for him. "I have no use for her. And she'll just be in the way even after the other mage skulks out of town. Women like her are ... problematic."

"Then I'll take my pay and my new toy and be on my way, before all this starts to come to a head." The stranger took his hat off briefly to wave away a mosquito, and the Preacher saw a long, jagged scar across his left temple. It had the startling whiteness common to wounds caused by spellcraft, and the Paulist shuddered to think what kind of battle had left this unbeliever with damage like that.

"Then let's go collect both of them. This way." The Preacher led the scarred magician to an outbuilding a few yards behind the saloon, and around to a door that was hidden from sight behind stacks of scrap wood. Beyond the door was a dark stairway leading into the forgotten root cellar that he had discovered when he first came to town. He stood aside and let the man with the scar precede him into the dark of the shack. The mage made gesture in front of the pair; a small cool flame appeared and illuminated the steps into the darkness.

"You'll forgive me if I don't trust you behind me, padre." The stranger motioned the Paulist to lead the way, "And don't mind the light — it's not hot."

The Paulist eyed the conjuration with hesitation. While the book said that you shouldn't allow a witch to stay, others said that was mistranslation and that witches and mages posed a threat that should be dealt with far harsher punishment than being driven out of areas the Church was gaining sway. He finally stepped forward, and the two descended until an old iron-bound door marked the entrance to the cellar.

The holy man pulled out a thick iron key from the pouch at his waist and opened the lock keeping Petra imprisoned.

"Don't worry," he said, "She's tied up good."

•   •   •

Cal sat in the middle of the meeting room, surrounded by Franklin and a few other men while the town council gathered. The Preacher had left them almost as soon as the group chivvied Cal into the meeting hall, and with a dark scowl had promised to return for the "trial" after his morning prayers. Cal felt slightly nauseous — the effects of the silver manacles was subtle but effective at keeping magic users from breaking free. As more and more people filled the room, Cal kept looking around for Petra, hoping she'd show up and put an end to the nonsense. While he waited, he listened to the conversation Alton was having with Mayor Tom.

"We should have listened to the Preacher!" The sheriff was keeping his voice down, not wanting to make his boss look bad but clearly reminding him that they had been on opposite sides of an earlier discussion. "Like he said, these mages just want our womenfolk and mean us no good."

The mayor was conciliatory. "Now Alton, we all agreed that sending to Peregrine House was the right plan. The Preacher offered his help only if we'd agree to let him start a chapter house here, and the Mages did cut their fee in half."

"Who cares about half a fee? That Cal Oakenflame took Petra's whole virtue!"

"I'm not sure things got that far, Alton. And we still don't know what happened. Now look, I know that Preacher showing off that gold bar said it would be ours after a year of establishing the chapter house got a lot of folk around here interested, but the Paulists also have a reputation for ... taking control ... That gave a lot of us pause, as well. Do you want to move from being sheriff to making sure everybody is sitting in their houses doing nothing on sabbat?"

Alton scowled, but said nothing more. Mayor Tom called the group to order, and slowly things went silent. "Now Mage Oakenflame, do we have your word that you'll stay nice and relaxed until we figure this out, so we can take that silver off you?"

•   •   •

Petra heard voices on the stairs and again debated calling out. But she concluded again that whoever put her in there and tied her up (badly), would likely be the one to hear her. She pondered and finally picked a different strategy.

She waited.

With a bar of gold in each of her clenched fists.

She closed her eyes so she wouldn't be blinded if whoever was coming had a torch or lantern, and when she heard the scrape of a key in the lock, she pushed herself into the pot where she might avoid being seen when they opened the door. She'd chased coyotes with rocks, this shouldn't be too much different. She just needed to be sure not to hit anybody too hard in case they weren't her kidnappers.

The door swung inward, and only a little light spilled in, so the outline of the first person to enter was clear.

Thunk.

Then the person was on the ground, and Petra was face to face with his companion.

The Preacher! And by the look on his face, he wasn't there to rescue her.

She made a split-second decision and hurled one of the gold bars at the Paulist's head. He cursed and ducked, and she sprinted past him into the stairway, one shiny bar of metal still clutched in her hand. She kicked the door shut behind her, barely registering that the key was still in the lock on the outside of the room.

Well then, he'll just have to wait with his friend until we sort this mess out. The thought flitted through her mind with just enough clarity that she twisted the key and pulled it out, leaving the two men in the very situation they had hoped to find her in. Then she dashed up the stairs, blinking as she emerged into the light and got her bearings.

The old shed behind the saloon! The one they didn't let the kids play near because it was old and nobody much cared to fix it up or tear it down. Petra could hear pounding on the door behind her and saw a small gathering at the meeting hall across the dusty main street. Figuring she'd find the town leaders there, she settled her hat on her head and headed over, a heart full of fury and a fist full of gold.

•　　　•　　　•

Cal felt immediately better once Alton had unwound the lightweight chain from his wrists. He didn't give the room the satisfaction of rubbing his wrists or shaking his head to clear it, but he certainly wanted to. The mayor continued.

"While we wait for the Preacher, why don't you tell us about last night? We couldn't find you anywhere to talk about that wanted poster ruse we were working on, then you showed up this morning and Petra was gone."

Cal went over the night's events, even detailing the reason he'd had to snatch up Petra to get through the protections of the *Mudders Map* on the bandit camp. He didn't tell them about the ring he'd given Petra, just that he'd set her up to escape on Copper.

There were some mutterings when he described grabbing Petra up, but the mayor put a stop to them with a look. "We asked him here to help, we can't fault his methods."

"Then where is she?" Somebody shouted, "Just because he says he sent her home don't mean he did! She might be there in the bandit camp right now, having to service those heathens!"

Another called out, "We want to hear from the Preacher. What does his book say about all this?"

Cal noticed that Alton had looked directly at each speaker right before they spoke up. Was he signaling them? The sheriff looked toward another corner of the room, and this time Cal caught a slight nod just before a woman stepped forward.

"So where is she, mage?" she spit at his feet, "Where is our Petra?" The woman was familiar, but Cal hadn't been in town long enough to place her.

There was a bang from behind the crowd and a stomping of boots that was somehow more feminine than boot stomping normally was. Another bang as the door that had been slammed open was slammed shut and a figure in a broad hat and gingham dress stamped her way to the front of the crowd.

"I'm right here, Sarah Gooding, not like you'd be happy to see me after what I saw last night in that camp!" The other woman flushed and retreated back into the crowd, muttering darkly that she had no idea what Petra was talking about.

Petra stood next to Cal, and he looked at her in astonishment. Where had she come from? Her dress was muddy and she had cobwebs strung from her hat. Wisps of her hair crossed her face, and she irritably tucked them back up under the brim. He found that oddly endearing, wisely choosing not to say anything about her appearance as he stood from the chair he'd been in.

"I think," Cal murmured, "You may want to tell everybody what you've been up to."

"I've been up to saving myself from that Preacher," Petra whispered back, "Or at least, I think so. He unlocked the door where they had stuck me, so I figured he was in on it." She held up the iron key she'd used to turn the tables on her captors and turned to the crowd around them.

"That Preacher man was in with the bandits!" There was a collective gasp, and Cal noted that the woman called Sarah Gooding was quietly leaving, unremarked by the crowd. Seeing that, Cal turned his gaze onto Alton to see what he could see, while Petra continued.

"See this?" She held up her other hand so the bar of gold joined the key above her head. "Recognize it?"

27

The mayor approached carefully, and she handed him the bar. He traced the stamped impression carefully. Then sighed. "Petra, did you steal this from the Preacher? It's got the Paulist mark on it and we know he carried one with him."

Petra whirled on him. "I did no such thing, Tom Biddleman. You know I'm no thief. There's a whole chest of these out under that old shed, which by the way is where he stuck me." She brushed a cobweb off her dress, suddenly aware of the state of her clothes even as they demonstrated her imprisonment. "Alton, you take this key and go fetch that Preacher right now. He has to answer for what's going on."

The lawman stepped forward, Cal watching him closely. "Right ... uh ... under that old shed, you said?"

"Yes I did, and I know you heard me. You go fetch him right now. And no need to be gentle." She rubbed her head under the hat. "He wasn't with me."

"I'll go too." Cal spoke up, and stood up, hoping that Petra's appearance would take the wind out of the idea that he was responsible for any shenanigans. "Just to be sure." Alton scowled, but nodded warily. Cal made sure that Aunt Lainie stepped forward to take charge of Petra in case the crowd got strange notions about her too, and then followed the sheriff out of the meeting house to the shed.

What met his eyes made his heart speed up. Another mage, recognizable by the bracelets he wore and the slight flicker of spirit that Cal could see stood on the end of the dusty street. He didn't know the other man, but would certainly know him again by the edge of scar he could see snaking from under the brim of the stranger's hat. And he definitely recognized the tingle around his wrists warning him that something harmful was brewing. Reflexively, he twitched his right wrist in the pattern to charge his own defenses.

"You cost me, Cal Oakenflame, you cost me dear!" The other man shouted the words, as if for an audience.

Cal faced the scarred man, squinting in the bright light. He was vaguely aware of Alton moving slowly away from where the two magick users squared off. Cal was also aware that the people inside the meeting house now stood crowded on its long veranda. He could see glints of sun off the windows of the saloon, and hoped the people inside were pulling curtains and staying well back from the glass.

"I don't know you, so what could I have cost you?" He said the words in a normal voice — he'd always hated his fellow mages' flair for drama around townsfolk.

"That gold should have been mine! That girl should have been mine." The scarred man pointed, and Cal looked to see Petra standing at the rail of the meeting house, one hand gripping her aunt's arm, the other clenched at her side.

"I don't think she belongs to anybody," Cal replied dryly, "And we'll decide who owns the gold. Why don't you be on your way, Stranger?"

"Not until I. GET. PAID!" The stranger's voice rose as his arm lashed straight out in front of him and a lance of red-orange fire sped toward Cal's end of the street.

Cal ducked the blast, but a hair's-breadth too late to save his hat, which was whipped away by the casting. It was one of the more powerful offensive spells he'd encountered and must have cost the other mage a fair bit of his strength. But Cal saw the scarred man was rapidly preparing another and was still standing strong. Cal's ears were ringing from the sound of that much spirit being consumed, but his own reflexes kicked in.

That's the problem with using that much power, he thought, *you're too busy* controlling *that much power.* Six smaller conjurations flew from his own fingers, each accompanied by a different sound, a rapid succession of zinging explosions that left echoes bouncing between the buildings that lined the small street and caused the onlookers to cover their ears.

The wind seemed to have died down and an eerie silence fell, as if the whole town had gone still. Cal sucked in a dusty breath and braced himself for the next blast from the scarred magician, but it never came. Instead, the stranger at the end of the dusty avenue stood stiff and still, arm raised but never completing his next casting.

Slowly, he crumbled to the ground. The air shimmered, and a whirling dust devil whipped by an unseen wind moved across the body, gathered speed, and then was gone, along with any trace of the scarred mage.

Silence reigned.

Cal finally released the breath he was holding, and as if on cue the townsfolk of Harrison burst into a babble of noise. Petra was at his side, grabbing his hand to pull him off the street and toward the shade of the saloon's veranda.

Any hope he had of resting was quickly dashed when he realized she was pulling him past the building, toward the back.

"Now we can take care of that Preacher!" She pulled Cal along by the hand as she strode toward the abandoned shed. "He's gotta still be in there!" Cal stumbled and dropped Petra's hand to balance himself.

By the time he made it to the shed, she was standing there with her hands on her hips. "You coming or do I have to take care of him my own self?"

Cal saw the stairs leading down and pointed to the bottom. She whirled and cursed when she saw the shards of broken timber that had been a stout locked door when she'd seen it last. She didn't hesitate to grab Cal's hand again to pull him into the downward path. "He ain't getting away that easily!"

Petra was right. In the light of the glow Cal conjured (which was about as much strength as he had after the *Pistoletta* conjuration), they could see the Preacher sprawled out, a pool of dark liquid soaking into the cellar floor where he lay. The wound that had killed him was a tangled mess of blood and bone in his chest, and Cal could just barely see a flicker of spirit from the blast that had caused it. Whoever the stranger had been, he must have been incredibly powerful to use so many destructive workings in such a short period of time. Cal was frankly surprised that he was the one walking away from their duel.

Petra was doing something in the shadows, and he heard a grunt and a dragging sound from her direction. He looked away from the corpse and saw her dragging a small wooden box toward the stairs.

"Is that the Preacher's gold?"

"Nope, that's *our* gold. At least it is now."

"But the Paulists —"

"Looks like they just paid for the damage those bandits did to our town and my sheep."

Once again, Cal kept wisely silent.

Back in the light, Cal blinked to see the townsfolk gathered around Petra, who was standing over the gold with her arms crossed, clearly not willing to let just anybody relieve her of it. Alton and a few others had gone into the basement and were engaged in bringing the body of the Paulist preacher slowly up the stairs, a task made difficult because the damage to his body made it harder to carry in a normal way.

"No, I'll stand back when Mayor Tom gets here, and not a second before then." Petra's tone was firm. "I want to hear what he has to say for himself!"

The mayor appeared at the edge of the crowd and pushed his way to Petra's side. "Now Petra, what's this fuss?" He caught sight of the gold she was guarding. "And what in the name of holy things is that? Gold?" He bent to touch it, mindful of Petra's kicking range. "Paulist gold?" he traced the mark in the small ingot. "That ain't good."

"No, it isn't, Mayor. And I'll tell you why." Cal had his wits about him again and had pieced a couple of things together. "This is how those bandits could afford that conjuration up in the hills — there's no reason for sheep thieves to have that kind of cash." He had the crowd's full attention, but it was Petra's gaze he felt on him the most.

"How about telling me about the Preacher. When did he come here, and what did he say?"

Petra launched the explanation before the town leader could open his mouth. "He came here because he'd heard we had bandit problems. Promised that if we let him build a chapter house and accept his help, the monks would help keep us safe. Said we'd be a richer town because of it."

A townswoman interrupted, "He showed us one of them bars, said there'd be more when more people came to pray and needed food, and places to stay. All we needed to do was let them in."

Petra silenced her with a glare and continued as if nobody had said anything. "Most of us were against it, but some people," she eyed the tall lawman, "argued pretty heavy for letting 'em stay, saying we were too vulnerable, and the sheep thieves just proved their point. Others like Aunt Lainie said we should send for, well, I guess we sent for you."

"Preacher was none too pleased!" Another townsperson braved Petra's glare. "He said you mages were heathens! And that he couldn't ask St. Paul to intercede with the savior in heaven if we let you into town."

Cal was familiar with the threat. Although sparse in Lifor, the Paulist chapter houses and the mage's colleges were brushing up against each other more and more often. And not always with happy results. He spoke up.

"I can't prove this." The crowd grumbled but let him wave them to silence. "But I think that gold was meant to pay for the working that kept the bandit camp hidden. You said the Preacher came pretty soon after the raids started ... does that seem odd to any of you?"

There were nods. Cal noticed Alton edging toward the back of the crowd, but let the man go. If he was involved somehow, that would be Mayor Tom's problem. If the Paulists were working with a mage, especially one as powerful as the scarred stranger, to cause havoc in towns and then "rescue" them, he had to get back to Peregrine House as soon as he could to make a full report — an orb wouldn't be enough.

"Let's take this inside, shall we?" Cal asked.

Reluctantly Petra let one of the burlier townsmen hoist the chest up and carry it into the meeting house, but she hovered close and sat right down on top of it once it was back on the rough pine boards of the council room. "Finders keepers," she told the townfolk. "At least until the mayor tells me otherwise."

The crowd settled into the seats and benches scattered around, and Cal looked to the mayor. "First things first. I don't think they'll trouble you anymore, but somebody should go check out the bandit camp. Somebody who can use this." He pulled out a small pendulum. One of the **younger townsmen came forward.**

"I know how to use that," the young man said, somewhat nervously. "I'm Tac Dowser."

Cal looked to Petra, who nodded and said, "Tac and his family witched just about every well in Harrison, and done quite a few for other towns." She smiled warmly at the young man. "And if anybody can use that gadget, he can."

Cal caught himself being irked that she was speaking highly of the other man, but shook it off. She was just a country girl and he'd be riding away in a day — what business was it of his who she was sweet on? He felt better when he caught Petra's eye, and she had the decency to blush.

"No need for dowsing, I left a marker that this will track to." Cal settled his voice back to what he hoped was authority. "But he shouldn't go alone."

There was a moment of pause … then Mayor Tom, looking disgruntled, said, "Where's Alton? His posse should go out with Tac."

When nobody answered, he sighed and pointed to one of the men who had helped arrest Cal. "Alright, you get the posse together and find that camp!" Several men and one or two women gathered up whatever they had with them and walked out together — Cal assumed that was the Harrison posse.

He also was afraid of what they might find following that pendulum.

•　　　•　　　•

Cal was right to be concerned. The posse returned later that night, with a horror story.

Connected to the sigil Cal had drawn under the bed inside the hovel at the bandit camp, the pendulum had no problem leading the group of deputized townsfolk right to the place where the bad guys had been hiding out between raids on Harrison and other local towns. But according to one of the men, at one point they didn't need the charm to guide them.

"We could just follow our noses," said the deputy, a tall, solid young man with the clever name of Knack. He looked a little ill just talking about it. "There was blood and guts all over the place, like they had just ... exploded or something."

"And the flies!" Another deputy, a young blond woman barely out of her teens named Jinje, waved her hands to demonstrated. "Clouds of 'em. We could hear the buzzing before we saw the mess."

"But the strangest thing was —" Knack glanced at Jinje in annoyance for taking over his story.

The younger blond was undeterred. "We didn't find any heads!"

Cal shivered at that. This was looking darker and darker. But he had to wrap up things here before he could head back to Peregrine House to let his order know what he had found. He looked to Mayor Tom and Petra.

"I don't think they'll be bothering you anymore, do you, Mr. Mayor?"

"Ah, no. And with the gold that was ... er—"

"Left behind in payment." Petra was sticking her line of reasoning. "We can more than make up for our losses. And send the Paulists a polite 'thank you, but no thank you' note." She looked at Cal and smiled — he felt a very unmagelike blush overcome his face under her gaze. "Looks like the wizard here got the job done."

"Alright then." Cal settled his hat back on his head. "Looks like it's time for me to head out."

"I'll go get Copper saddled," said Petra, "meet me around the back of the stable." She was gone before Cal could protest that he didn't need the assistance. Oh well, let her do her thing.

He shook hands with Mayor Tom, with the posse members and other townsfolk, still half looking for the sheriff and the other woman who had been at the bandit camp. He never saw them, but left that up to the town leaders to worry about, or not. Nothing in the disappearance of a couple of people into the wilds of Lifor was any of his business.

He looked at the slow growing red and gold toward the west as he walked out to gather his horse. Neither he nor Copper minded riding at night, and if he could get even a few hours on the road before needing to make a cowboy camp he'd take it. He didn't see Petra or his horse as he moved around to the rear of the stable, and called out to see if they were in one of the stalls.

"In here, Mr. Magician!" Petra's voice came from a high-walled stall at the other end of the stable, and Cal crossed to that side of the building, the rich smell of molasses oats and fresh straw making him feel a little reluctant to be leaving already. He hadn't slept much and there was a cozy warmth in the barn that made him think of naps, warm blankets, and for some reason, somebody to share them with. A particular somebody in a gingham dress, perhaps.

There was no horse in the stall. But there was a thick flannel blanket, a country village meal of bread and cheese and wine arranged on it, and Petra sitting cross legged with a cup of wine already in her hand.

"You weren't really going to just ride off into the sunset, were you, cowboy?" Again, she was not the one blushing this time. "I don't usually feed strangers, but I thought you could do with a meal before hitting the trail."

Cal fumbled for words. "Oh, ah, well, I'll probably be back —"

"You'd better be." Petra reached up and took one of his wrists. When the ring on her finger clicked against the copper bracelet there was a short bright burst of energy that left Cal's entire body tingling. At least, that's what he was telling himself was the reason.

Petra laughed and pulled him down to sit next to her, looking him right in the eyes. Her cornflower blue eyes were like the eyes of a mother goddess and wild sprite all in one. "You aren't the only one with some magic." Her throaty chuckle pierced right to his heart, and other places. She kissed him first, then pushed him down onto the blanket.

It was delightful magic indeed.

ABOUT THE AUTHOR

Joshua Ramey-Renk has been writing and submitting and publishing for over *ahem cough* years. His fiction work has appeared in *DailyScienceFiction.com* and a variety of small press anthologies. He loves reader feedback and might be next to you in a café scribbling away in any one of a myriad of notebooks, scrapbooks, and journals. Joshua lives on the San Francisco Peninsula with his wife and two treat-addicted rescue dogs, Roadie and Pepper.

YOU MIGHT ALSO ENJOY

THE ALCHEMIST DAUGHTER
by Paul S. Moore

When a concoction of ethers channels a little of their magic properties to one location, inspiration springs to life.

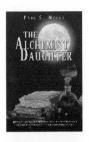

THE INN OF THE SEVEN STARS
by Kevin Beckett

A tale of an inn with good music, tasty food, strong beer ... and inadvertent necromancy.

SONGS OF A DEAD FOREST
by Travis Wade Beaty

Old songs can bring new life.

Available in digital and trade paperback editions from
Water Dragon Publishing
waterdragonpublishing.com

Milton Keynes UK
Ingram Content Group UK Ltd.
UKHW012222290324
440241UK00001B/34

9 781962 538435